Jellytoes

Misses the Bus

Written and Illustrated by
Andrew Barlow

MJS

Publishing
Group, LLC

Ben.
I hope you love
the new
book.

Manufactured in U.S.A.

10 9 8 7 6 5 4 3 2 1

ISBN: 0-9764336-0-5

This edition published by MJS Publishing Group, LLC. For sales information log on to www.mjspub.com.

Production by Ignite Communications & Design Inc., 544 Woodlawn Ave., Glencoe, Illinois 60022.

"Jellytoes" is a trademark of Andrew Barlow.

Larry and Barry waited at the corner outside of Jellytoes's house for the school bus. Jellytoes was still in bed! He was dreaming about the party his class was having at school.

He stopped in the kitchen for some breakfast.

His favorite! Chicken wings!

Jellytoes gobbled them all up.

Then he bounced out the door to catch the bus!

Larry and Barry giggled at their friend.

School Bus

Wow, look at him go!

Looks like he'll be late!

As he chased the bus, Jellytoes heard something in the bushes.

What's that?

CLUCK

CLUCK

CLUCK

First, there was one angry chicken.

Jellytoes raced the rest of the way home.
He went to the garage and peeked inside.

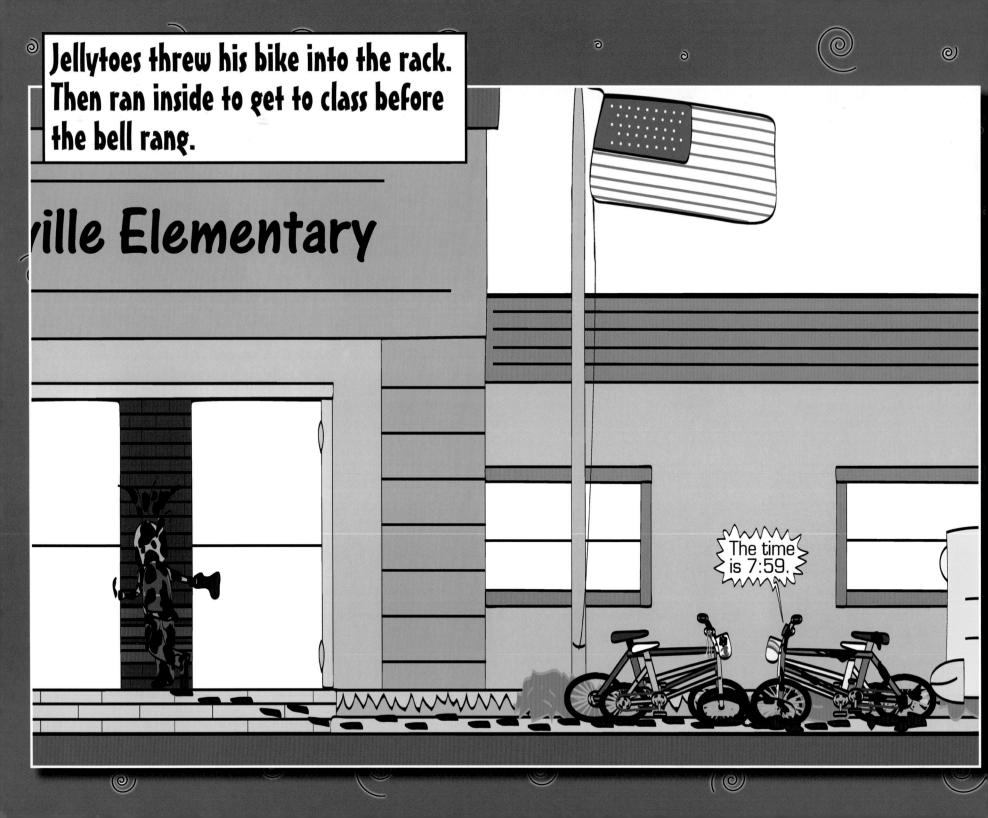

School was very important.
Jellytoes did not want to run late ever again.
Next time, you should slide in head first!
There won't be a next time.

ABOUT THE AUTHOR

Andrew Barlow is an author who makes his home in Carlisle, Iowa, and *Jellytoes Misses the Bus* is his first book. Andrew enjoys children—and had lots of fun throughout his own childhood. The ideas for some of Jellytoes's exploits come from things he, his brother, and their friends did when they were young. According to Andrew, Jellytoes is a typical kid who occasionally does things that might seem "brainless," but he always figures out what to do—sometimes with the help of his friends, sometimes on his own. In either case, it's always fun and it's always an adventure.

Watch for the next book in the Jellytoes series:

Jellytoes Goes Fishing.